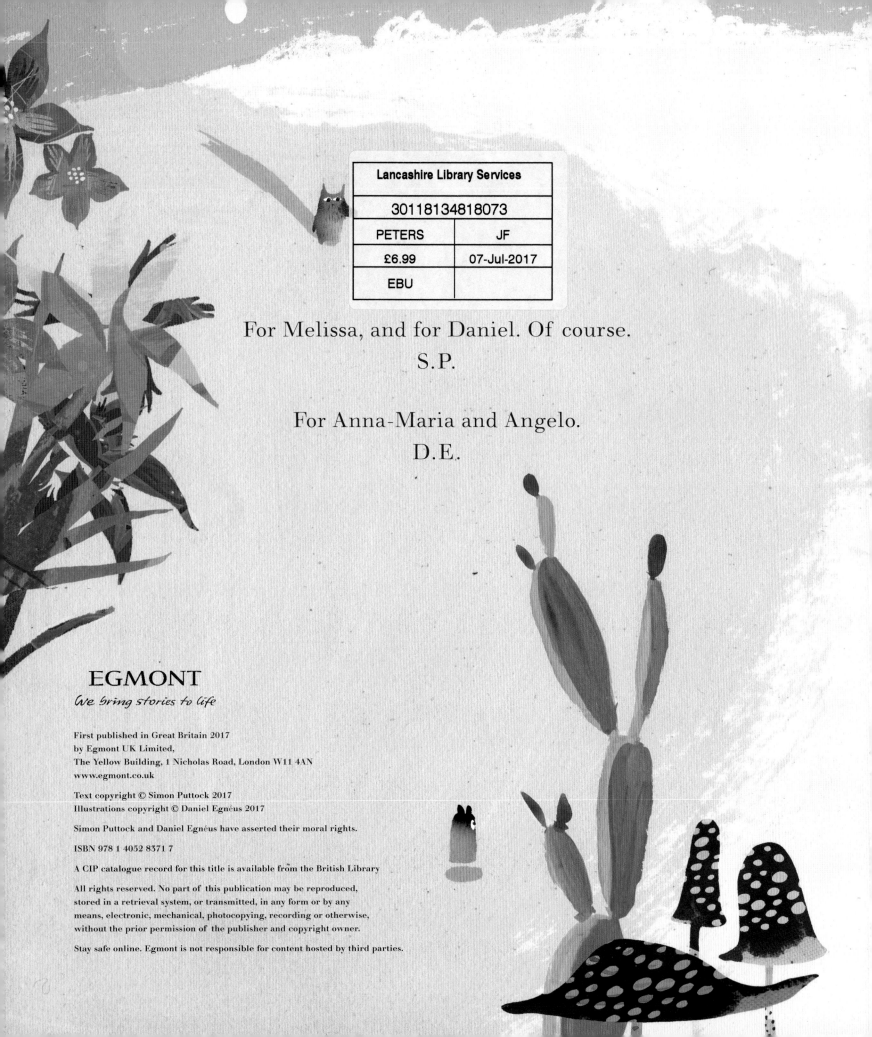

For Melissa, and for Daniel. Of course.
S.P.

For Anna-Maria and Angelo.
D.E.

EGMONT
We bring stories to life

First published in Great Britain 2017
by Egmont UK Limited,
The Yellow Building, 1 Nicholas Road, London W11 4AN
www.egmont.co.uk

Text copyright © Simon Puttock 2017
Illustrations copyright © Daniel Egnéus 2017

Simon Puttock and Daniel Egnéus have asserted their moral rights.

ISBN 978 1 4052 8371 7

A CIP catalogue record for this title is available from the British Library

The Thing

Simon Puttock
& Daniel Egnéus

EGMONT

The Thing lay where it had fallen,
not moving at all, not making a sound.

"What is it?" said someone passing by.

"And what does it do?"
asked another.

A third shrugged.

"Maybe it just is."

"Whatever it is," said a fourth,
"it's beautiful."

"Is it **alive?**" asked the first,
who was Cobble.

"Difficult to say," said Tummler,
who was next.

"It looks sort of . . .

. . . lonely,"
said Hummly,
the third one.

"We could stay and keep it
company," said the last one,
who was Roop.

So they all lay down beside the Thing that lay where it was,
not moving at all, not making a sound, and they slept.

In the morning, the Thing was just the same.

"Let's try talking to it." Hummly went right up close and shouted:

"Hullo!"

"Not like that," said Roop. "You're supposed to say

greetings!"

"Yes," said Tummler, "and,

we

come

in

peace!"

"Are you sure?" asked Cobble. "Because I thought
the Thing had come to us . . ."

But it didn't matter really, because the Thing
just lay where it was, not moving
at all, not making a sound.

"Hmm," said Cobble. "This could take a while."

"Let's build a shelter," said Tummler, "while we work this out."

"It could be a shelter for
the Thing, too," said Roop.

"Good idea," said Hummly.

They drew up a plan for a shelter,
both wonderful and grand.

People began to come from far and wide
to see the Thing that lay where it was,

not moving at all,

not making a sound.

Of course, they asked questions:

What is it?

Whose is it?

What does it **do?**

Can we have one, too?

"It isn't ours to give away," said Cobble.
"And besides, there's only one of it."

"We just sort of look after it," said Tummler.

"We keep the rain off it," Hummly explained.

"And we sit and think about it, too," said Roop.

So many people came to see the Thing
that soon it was like a **funfair:**

there were hot dog kiosks
and hamburger stands;

lemonade stalls and
tables of souvenirs for sale.

Everyone who came to see the Thing
took something away with them: a postcard,
or a little plastic model of the Thing;
a balloon or a button; a flag or a mug.

Someone set up a camera so that people
could watch it from the comfort of their homes.

Now the Thing was famous

all over the world.

But still, it just lay there;
just lay where it was, not moving at all,

not making a sound.

Not everyone liked
the Thing, of course.

Some people thought it was
too strange, or worrisome,
or possibly even dangerous.

"That Thing," they said,
"does not belong.

It
HAS
to GO."

All over the world, people began to argue **for** and **against** the Thing.

There was quite a lot of bad feeling.

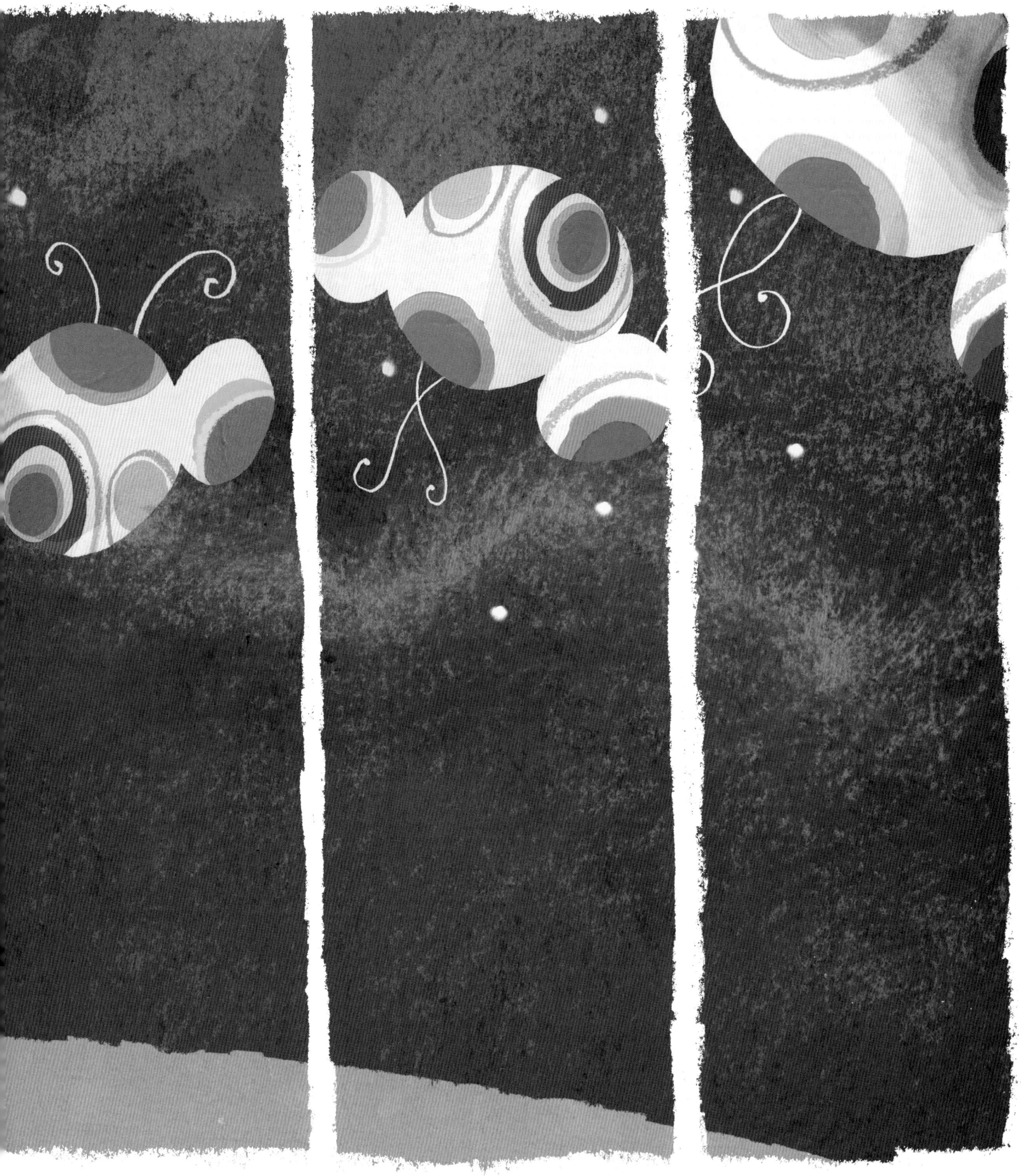

And then, one morning, without a sound,
the Thing was gone.

It had somehow un-fallen itself and
disappeared, almost as if it had never been.

People stopped coming.

After all, there was really
nothing more to see.

Some people said,
"How sad."

Some people said,
"Good riddance!"

The stalls and stands, the kiosks
and cafes all closed down.

The camera was switched off.

"I still don't know what it was," said Hummly, "but I'll miss it."

"Yes," said Cobble. "It has all been very mysterious."

"Before the Thing came,"
said Tummler, "we were strangers."

Roop smiled.

"And now we are friends."

They stayed to watch the sun go down, and then, because
there were **things** that they really must be getting on with,
they hugged each other happily and, with promises to meet again soon . . .

. . . they went their separate ways.

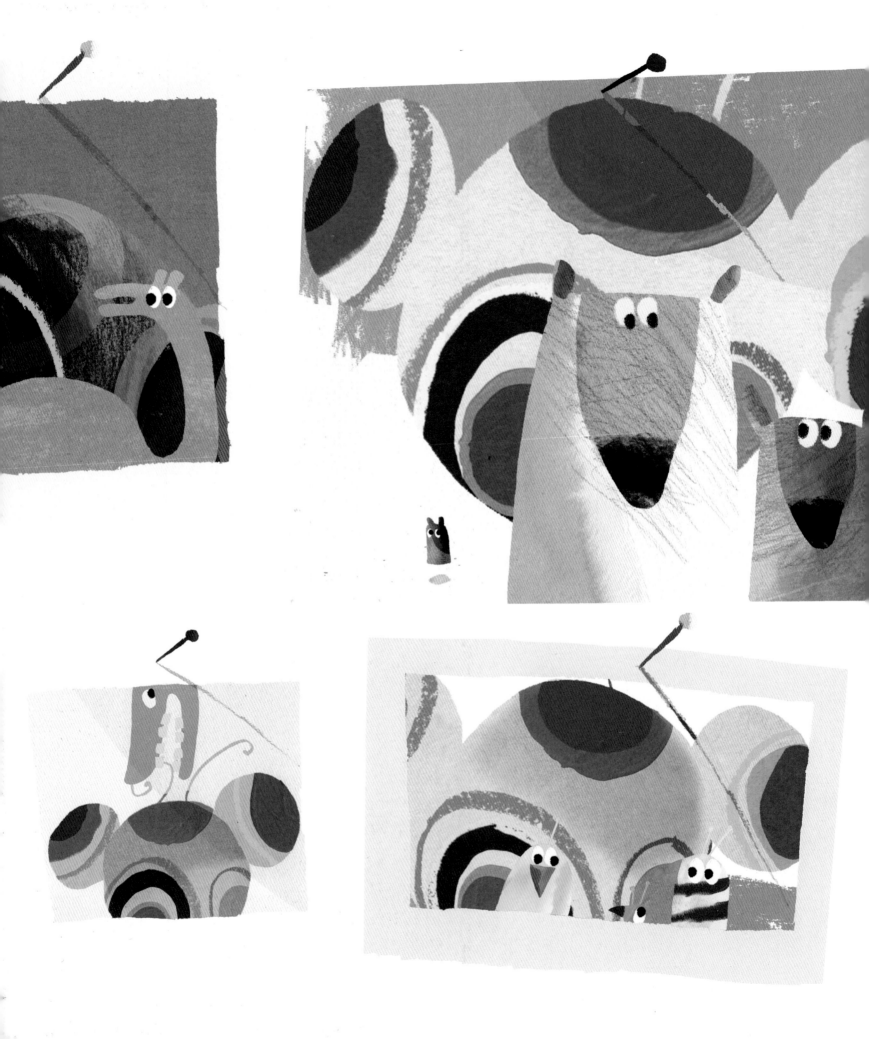